Patchwork

Feelings

Written by Felicia Law
Illustrated by Paula Knight

NORWOOD HOUSE PRESS

Chicago, Illinois

DEAR CAREGIVER

The **Patchwork** series is a whimsical collection of books that integrate poetry to reinforce primary concepts among emergent readers. You might consider these modern-day nursery rhymes that are relevant for today's children. For example, rather than a Miss Muffet sitting on a tuffet, eating her curds and whey, your child will encounter a Grandma and Grandpa dancing a Samba, or a big sister who knows how to make rocks skim and the best places to swim.

Not only do the poetry and prose within the **Patchwork** books help children broaden their understanding of the concepts and recognize key words, the rhyming text helps them develop phonological awareness—an underlying skill necessary for success in transitioning from emergent to conventional readers.

As you read the text, invite your child to help identify the words that rhyme, start and end with similar sounds, or find the words connected to the pictures. The pictures in these books feature illustrations resembling the technique of torn-paper collage. The artwork can inspire young artists to experiment with torn-paper to create images and write their own poetry.

Above all, the most important part of the reading experience is to have fun and enjoy it!

Sincerely,

Shannon Cannon

Shannon Cannon, Ph.D.
Literacy Consultant

Norwood House Press • P.O. Box 316598 • Chicago, Illinois 60631
For more information about Norwood House Press please visit our website at
www.norwoodhousepress.com or call 866-565-2900.

LIBRARY OF CONGRESS CATALOGING-IN-PUBLICATION DATA
Law, Felicia.
   Feelings / by Felicia Law ; illustrated by Paula Knight.
      pages cm. -- (Patchwork)
   Summary: Torn paper collages and simple, rhyming text portray children experiencing various emotions, from greed over jelly doughnuts to fear of nighttime shadows. Includes a word list.
   ISBN 978-1-59953-712-2 (library edition : alk. paper) -- ISBN 978-1-60357-810-3 (ebook)
[1. Stories in rhyme. 2. Emotions--Fiction.] I. Knight, Paula, illustrator. II. Title.
   PZ8.3.L3544Fee 2015
   [E]--dc23
                                   2014047198

274N—062015
Manufactured in the United States of America in North Mankato, Minnesota.

Look at me!

Boom! Boom!
Beat the drum
I'm the greatest!
I'm the king!
I'm the best
At everything!

See me marching
Here I come
I'm the leader
Beat the drum

3

Hungry

Munching
And crunching
Stuffing donuts in
Licking the jam
That dribbles
Down my chin

Mom says, don't be greedy
You'll make yourself ill

Surely she knows
I've got a tummy to fill!

4

Upset

My bike hit a stone
   And I was thrown
      To the ground and landed
    With a
         thump

Then the naughty stone
    Bruised my bone
      So it's pink and sore
     From the
       bump

Now the bump's begun to bleed
   So I need
     A kiss and cuddle
    What a
        chump!

Shopping tantrum

He doesn't want carrots
He doesn't want greens
He doesn't want tomatoes
Or stringy beans

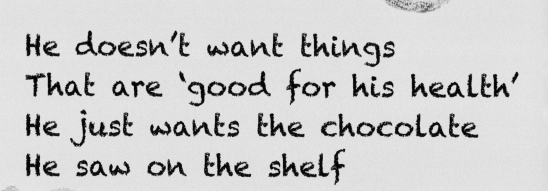

He doesn't want things
That are 'good for his health'
He just wants the chocolate
He saw on the shelf

8

She loves me

My pet bunny loves me
She's my greatest fan
She tells me this quite often
When I'm spooning out her bran

She tells me she loves me
When I'm brushing through her coat
She says she cares about me
When she's munching on her oats!

11

12

Resting on the Rug

Shhh! It's quiet
Down here. Hush! Shush!

We try to lie still
So no-one comes near
They tiptoe round the carpet

"Shhh! They're resting
Don't make a noise
Don't touch a foot or a paw."

But they don't see us peeping
We're really not sleeping

Hooray for presents

Hooray, it's my birthday
And there's a big surprise
Hiding in this present

I can't wait to see inside!

15

It's mine

It's mine
It's mine
I saw it first

It's mine
It's mine
You'll break it

It's mine
It's mine
I want it back

It's mine
It's mine
I'LL TAKE IT!

16

17

A sad goodbye

I didn't want to leave you
I didn't want to go
I didn't want to make
    you sad
Tried not to let it show

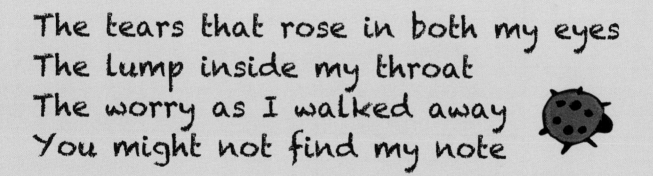

The tears that rose in both my eyes
The lump inside my throat
The worry as I walked away
You might not find my note

    In which I wrote 'I love you
    But I have school this afternoon
    And though I have to go now
    Wait here - I'll be back soon'

Night fright

The shadows creep across the wall
They float around my head
They climb across my blankets
They slink beneath my bed

They wriggle in the curtains
They creep along the hem

But they don't come any closer
They know I'm watching them!

This book includes these concept words:

- bed
- blanket
- bump
- chin
- chocolate
- donut
- drum
- foot
- fright
- good
- greedy
- head

jam   present   tantrum

kiss   quiet   tears

love   sad   tummy

naughty   shadow

paw   surprise